The Human Under My Bed

and

King for the Day

Written by
Mignonne Gunasekara

Illustrated by
Irene Renon

The Human Under My Bed

and

King for the Day

Level 11 – Lime

Helpful Hints for Reading at Home

The focus phonemes (units of sound) used throughout this series are in line with the order in which your child is taught at school. This offers a consistent approach to learning whether reading at home or in the classroom.

HERE ARE SOME COMMON WORDS THAT YOUR CHILD MIGHT FIND TRICKY:

water	where	would	know	thought	through	couldn't
laughed	eyes	once	we're	school	can't	our

TOP TIPS FOR HELPING YOUR CHILD TO READ:

- Encourage your child to read aloud as well as silently to themselves.
- Allow your child time to absorb the text and make comments.
- Ask simple questions about the text to assess understanding.
- Encourage your child to clarify the meaning of new vocabulary.

This book focuses on developing independence, fluency and comprehension. It is a lime level 11 book band.

The Human Under My Bed

Written by
Mignonne Gunasekara

Illustrated by
Irene Renon

Chapter One

Myrtle was convinced that there was a human under her bed. She probably shouldn't have stayed up late to watch that scary film with her older cousins. She couldn't get the idea out of her head.

"Oh, sweetheart," said Mama Monster. "Humans don't exist!"

It was no good. Myrtle wasn't listening. She was too busy squeezing glow sticks into her bookcase.

"How can you sleep with all this light?" asked Papa Monster, poking his head round the bedroom door.

"I can't sleep," said Myrtle. "But that's the plan."

She stepped back to admire her handiwork. Now she could finally climb into bed.

"There is absolutely nothing under your bed," said Mama. "We promise."

"There's nothing when you look now," said Myrtle. "But in the middle of the night – that's when they come out!"

"Please get some sleep tonight, Myrtle," said Mama. "It's been a week! You must be tired."
"A growing monster needs all the sleep she can get," said Papa sternly.

"The human won't be sleeping," muttered Myrtle as she pulled a head torch out from under her pillow. "So I can't sleep either."
"Oh, Myrtle," sighed Mama as she stood up.
"We'll see you in the morning," said Papa, kissing Myrtle's forehead. Mama kissed her next, and then the two of them backed out of the door.

Papa was about to pull the door shut when Myrtle called out.

"No," she said. "Leave it open!"

Papa hesitated but did as Myrtle asked. He then reached over to turn off Myrtle's bedroom light, but when he saw the look on Myrtle's face, he decided to leave it on.

"Thank you," said Myrtle.

Papa and Mama slowly turned and left, but Myrtle was still sat up in bed. She looped her head torch around her head and turned it on. With the glow sticks, head torch, and her light on, Myrtle's room was brightly lit.

"No humans are going to get me tonight!" thought Myrtle.

Chapter Two

Before she knew it, it was morning and her eyes were starting to twitch. Every little noise in the night had made her jump and she was sick of it. She hadn't slept a wink! At school, Myrtle had bags under her eyes and staying awake in lessons had become a struggle.

She was super grumpy, and everything her teachers said went in one ear and straight out the other. She finally ended up nodding off in the middle of her history lesson. Her teacher didn't notice, but Myrtle was fed up. "Enough is enough!" she thought.

"I am going to have to take matters into my own hands and catch this human once and for all! Then I can finally get a good night's sleep. But how can I do that?"

Just then, an idea popped into Myrtle's head. She knew what she had to do.

Myrtle set to work the minute she got home from school. First stop was Papa's shed, where she picked up a big bucket and some rope. Then she went to the kitchen, where she raided the snack cupboard for sweets. She had heard that humans loved to eat sweets, so what better treat to use for her trap?

Myrtle was struggling to carry her trap materials upstairs when she dropped the bucket with a clang. "Myrtle?" called Mama from the living room. "What are you doing?" "Nothing!" yelled Myrtle. She knew her parents would think she was being silly. She would have to wait for them to fall asleep before she carried out her plan.

Myrtle shoved the bucket, rope and sweets into her wardrobe and sat back. She looked around her room for the last piece of her trap. She needed something to prop up the bucket. Her eyes finally landed on her Spelling Wasp trophy.

"A-ha!" said Myrtle. "That will do the trick!"

She was just about to pick the trophy up when she heard her parents laying the table in the dining room below her. "Dinner's ready!" bellowed Papa from downstairs. Myrtle had been so busy preparing her trap that she had forgotten all about dinner.

"I'll be right back, human," thought Myrtle. "Just you wait."

Chapter Three

At the dinner table, Mama and Papa watched as Myrtle ate her food as quickly as she possibly could. She was in a hurry to get back to her room. "Oh dear," whispered Mama, so that only Papa could hear.

"She's at breaking point," Papa whispered back.

"All done!" declared Myrtle, holding up her empty plate.

"Oh," started Mama.

"Can I be excused, please?" asked Myrtle.

"I suppose s-"

"Thank you!" yelled Myrtle over her shoulder as she disappeared out through the dining room door.

"Also, I don't need tucking in tonight!"

"You don't?" asked Mama. "What about the humans?"

"I'm not worried about them anymore!" said Myrtle, her voice drifting in from the landing. The next thing Mama and Papa heard was Myrtle's bedroom door closing.

"Well," said Papa. "That wasn't weird at all."

"I hope she really means that," said Mama. "Because there is nothing under her bed!"

Back in her room, Myrtle was setting up her trap. She had tied the rope to the trophy and used it to prop the bucket up. She tossed a handful of sweets under the bucket, picked up the other end of the rope, and climbed into bed.

"And now, I wait," said Myrtle.

The hours ticked by, but there was no sign of the human.

"Come on..." mumbled Myrtle, as her eyelids grew heavier.

Her head started to droop closer to her pillow. She tried to fight it, but it wasn't long before she was fast asleep. All those sleepless nights had finally caught up with her.

Chapter Four

When Myrtle woke up, the sweets had disappeared from her trap, but there was no human in sight!

"That pesky human!" thought Myrtle. "It got away!"

She'd get it next time. She just had to stay awake long enough!

That night, Myrtle set her trap up again. And just as she'd done before, she climbed into bed and waited. But she wouldn't fall asleep this time. She had a bag of spicy crisps with her, and every time she felt sleepy, she popped one in her mouth.

It got later and later, but nothing happened. "Not again," thought Myrtle.
She was nearly ready to give up when she heard a scuffling sound. The human was coming! She jumped up on her bed, held the rope tight and got ready to spring into action. The scuffling sound got louder and louder, until...
A dodo bird appeared from under Myrtle's bed! It scurried over to the sweets and started gobbling them up.

"There's no human after all!" exclaimed Myrtle. "It was just a silly dodo this whole time!"

Myrtle scooped it up and took it to her parents' room. They grumbled as Myrtle tried to wake them up. When they saw the dodo, they sat up straight in bed.

"What is that?" they gasped.

"The human under my bed!" said Myrtle. "Can we keep it?"

The Human Under My Bed

1.   What did Myrtle squeeze into her bookcase?

2.   What lesson did Myrtle nod off in?

3.   What did Myrtle take from Papa's shed?

    (a)   A big bucket and some rope

    (b)   A brush and dustpan

    (c)   A light bulb

4.   Why did Myrtle eat spicy crisps?

5.   How do you think Myrtle felt about there being a human under her bed? How would you feel if you thought something was under your bed?

King for the Day

Written by
Mignonne Gunasekara

Illustrated by
Irene Renon

Chapter One

When Boris grew up, he wanted to be the
king. If he were king, he would be able to do
whatever he wanted, whenever he wanted.
No one could tell him what to do because he
would be the most powerful person around!

Kings didn't have bedtimes, or homework, and that was the kind of life Boris wanted.
At breakfast, he decided to lay out his plans for his brothers and sisters. He had already written a list of the things that he planned on doing, which he rolled out all the way down the middle of the table.

"A-ha-hem," said Boris. "I, Boris the Brilliant, hereby announce my royal plans."

Nobody looked up from their bowls of cereal, but this did not put Boris off. He began to read out his list.

"I will build a grand palace," he declared. "It will have a water park in the garden. A slide will lead straight out of my bedroom and into the pool."

"I will have a pet mammoth," continued Boris. "I will ride it everywhere."

"Mammoths are extinct," pointed out his sister, Doris. "That's what makes them special enough for a king," said Boris. "I will make some scientists bring one back to life, just for me."

"All my subjects will bring me gifts on my birthday – and I will have a second birthday, just for good measure!"

"That's quite extreme," said Boris's other sister, Iris.

"That's how it works," replied Boris. "The king or queen gets two birthdays. Look it up. I will also play video games all day and eat desserts for every meal."

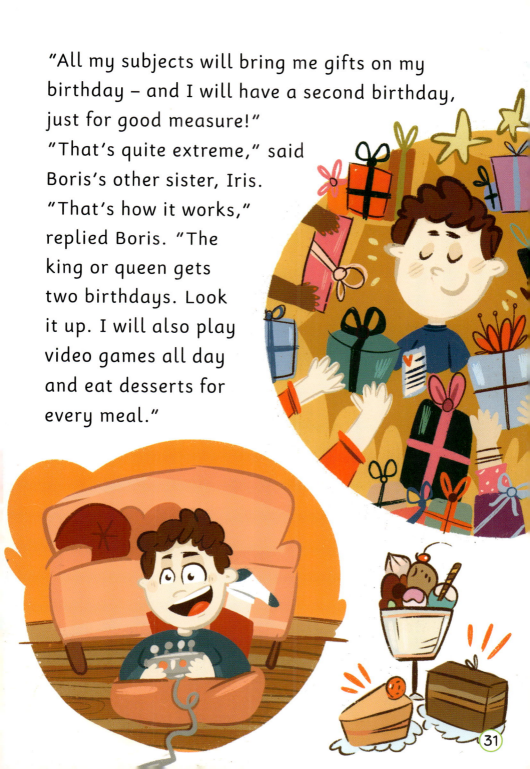

"That doesn't sound healthy at all!" said Doris. Boris's sisters turned back to their breakfast, thinking he was finally finished. But he had just been getting started. Boris ended up going on... and on... and on... until everyone but Boris himself was very annoyed.

Then his older brother, Morris, got an idea. If it worked, it would hopefully make Boris stop talking about this kind of thing for good.
"That all sounds great," said Morris. "But don't you want to be a king that's respected by his subjects?"
Boris stopped. He thought for a minute.

"What do you mean?" he finally asked.
"A good king needs to look after his kingdom properly," explained Morris. "And that means taking responsibility for things."
Boris didn't like the sound of that. It sounded like a lot of work, which was the opposite of what he wanted.

"If you want to be a proper king, that's what you'll need to do," said Morris. "In fact, you should try to be king for the day, to see if you're ready for the job."

"Of course I'm ready for the job!" exclaimed Boris.

"You are going to have to prove it," said Morris.

"How about..." mused Morris. "You can be in charge of everything our family needs to do today!"

"Everything?" asked Boris.

This all sounded a little bit scary to Boris. Morris, on the other hand, was really starting to enjoy himself.

"Of course, if that's too much for you to handle..." taunted Morris.

"No," said Boris. "I can do it!"

"Good," said Morris. "Your first job is to make sure everyone here does their bit to clean up after breakfast."

Boris looked down the table at all his brothers and sisters.

"Um, um..." stuttered Boris. "We need to do the washing up and wipe the table."

"Good," said Morris. "Who is going to do what?"

The twins, Mavis and Elvis, were only five. What could they do?

"Could the twins wipe the table while the rest of us take it in turns to wash the dishes?" asked Boris.

"Good idea," replied Morris.

Chapter Two

The children followed Boris's plan, until breakfast was fully cleared up.

"Now that's done, there's another task you have to sort out," said Morris.

"What task is that?" asked Boris.

"Shopping," said Morris. The word shook Boris to his core.

"No..." he whispered.

"Yes," said Morris. "You need to be in charge of our grocery shopping for the week. Use this."

Morris handed Boris a shopping list. It had eggs, milk, cleaning supplies, and several other everyday things on it. It would be boring, but it could be an easy win to prove he would be a good king.

"Ok," said Boris. "Let's go."

All the children made their way to Morris's car and he drove them to the local supermarket.

It was busy, and Boris just wanted to find everything on the list and leave as quickly as possible. But every five minutes, one of his brothers or sisters would ask him if they could buy something useless! They finally finished the shopping and went home. Boris was exhausted.

Chapter Three

Boris couldn't wait to get into bed and rest. He was walking to his bedroom when he heard Morris calling him.

"Oh, Boris?" said Morris. "We have a problem we'd like you to solve."

"What could they possibly want now?" thought Boris. He walked around the house looking for Morris, until he found himself in the twins' bedroom.

Morris was holding a stuffed monkey as he stood in between Mavis and Elvis.

"The twins both want to play with this toy," said Morris. "Who should get it?"

"Can't they play together?" asked Boris. "You know... share?"

Elvis and Mavis started to protest but Morris shushed them.

"Excellent decision," said Morris. He handed one of the monkey's paws to Mavis, and the other to Elvis. "While you're here, Boris, you can do your final task of the day."

"There's more?" wailed Boris.

"Just one more thing, I promise," said Morris. "You just have to get these two to go to sleep."

"Wait..." said Boris.

"I'm leaving you to it," said Morris as he walked out of the door. "Good luck!"

Boris turned to look at Mavis and Elvis. They were wide awake. More awake than Boris had ever seen them before.

"Get into bed," pleaded Boris.

"You have to use the magic word!" said Mavis.

"Please?" begged Boris.

"Alright," said Elvis. "But only because you asked so nicely."

He and Mavis climbed into their beds, but they didn't lie down.

"What are you doing?" asked Boris.

"You said to get into bed," giggled Elvis. "But you didn't say we had to sleep!"

Mavis started to laugh, and Elvis soon joined in.

"Go to sleep!" barked Boris, as he marched out of their bedroom. But they were still giggling! Boris slumped in front of their door. It looked like it was going to be a long night. The minutes passed and Boris was losing his mind with boredom. When Boris was finally certain that they'd fallen asleep, he tiptoed across the landing and down the stairs.

It was finally the end of the day and Boris was very tired. The minute he solved one problem, two more would pop up in its place! He shuffled into the living room and collapsed on the sofa.

"Maybe I don't really want to be king after all," mumbled Boris from under the sofa cushions.

Morris smiled to himself.

King for the Day

1.   What did Boris want to put in the garden of his palace?

2.   What pet did Boris want?

3.   What was Boris's first job as king?

4.   What did the twins both want to play with?

   (a)   A stuffed monkey

   (b)   A toy dog

   (c)   A cuddly bear

5.   How was Boris feeling at the end of the day? Do you think you would be a good king or queen?

©2020 **BookLife Publishing Ltd.**
King's Lynn, Norfolk PE30 4LS

ISBN 978-1-83927-028-4

The Human Under My Bed & King for the Day
Written by Mignonne Gunasekara
Illustrated by Irene Renon

An Introduction to BookLife Readers...

Our Readers have been specifically created in line with the London Institute of Education's approach to book banding and are phonetically decodable and ordered to support each phase of the Letters and Sounds document.

Each book has been created to provide the best possible reading and learning experience. Our aim is to share our love of books with children, providing both emerging readers and prolific page-turners with beautiful books that are guaranteed to provoke interest and learning, regardless of ability.

BOOK BAND GRADED using the Institute of Education's approach to levelling.

PHONETICALLY DECODABLE supporting each phase of Letters and Sounds.

EXERCISES AND QUESTIONS to offer reinforcement and to ascertain comprehension.

BEAUTIFULLY ILLUSTRATED to inspire and provoke engagement, providing a variety of styles for the reader to enjoy whilst reading through the series.

AUTHOR INSIGHT:
MIGNONNE GUNASEKARA

Despite being BookLife Publishing's newest recruit, Mignonne Gunasekara has already written fourteen books about everything from starter science and disastrous deaths throughout history to dinosaurs.
Born in Sri Lanka, Mignonne has always been drawn to stories, whether they are told through literature, film or music. After studying Biomedical Science at King's College London, Mignonne completed a short course in screenwriting at the National Centre for Writing in Norwich, during which she explored writing scripts for the different mediums of film, theatre and radio.

This book focuses on developing independence, fluency and comprehension. It is a lime level 11 book band.